FOREST FEELINGS

NANDO THE NEWT FEELS NERVOUS

by Megan Atwood
illustrated by Carissa Harris

Tools for Parents & Teachers

Grasshopper Books enhance imagination and introduce the earliest readers to fiction with fun storylines and illustrations. The easy-to-read text supports early reading experiences with repetitive sentence patterns and sight words.

Before Reading

- Discuss the cover illustration. What do they see?
- Look at the picture glossary together. Discuss the words.

Read the Book

- Read the book to the child, or have him or her read independently.
- "Walk" through the book and look at the illustrations. Who is the main character? What is happening in the story?

After Reading

- Prompt the child to think more. Ask: Nando feels nervous. How do we know? What does he say and do that show he is nervous?

Grasshopper Books are published by Jump!
5357 Penn Avenue South
Minneapolis, MN 55419
www.jumplibrary.com

Library of Congress Cataloging-in-Publication Data

Names: Atwood, Megan, author.
Harris, Carissa, illustrator.
Title: Nando the newt feels nervous / by Megan Atwood; illustrated by Carissa Harris.
Description: Minneapolis, MN: Jump!, Inc., 2024.
Series: Forest feelings | Includes index.
Audience: Ages 7–10.
Identifiers: LCCN 2023029076 (print)
LCCN 2023029077 (ebook)
ISBN 9798889969693 (hardcover)
ISBN 9798889969709 (paperback)
ISBN 9798889969716 (ebook)
Subjects: CYAC: Worry—Fiction. | Newts—Fiction.
Tail—Fiction. LCGFT: Animal fiction. | Picture books.
Classification: LCC PZ7.A8952 Nan 2024 (print)
LCC PZ7.A8952 (ebook)
DDC [E] —dc23
LC record available at https://lccn.loc.gov/2023029076
LC ebook record available at https://lccn.loc.gov/2023029077

Editor: Jenna Gleisner
Direction and Layout: Molly Ballanger
Illustrator: Carissa Harris

Printed in the United States of America at Corporate Graphics in North Mankato, Minnesota.

Table of Contents

A Nervous Tale

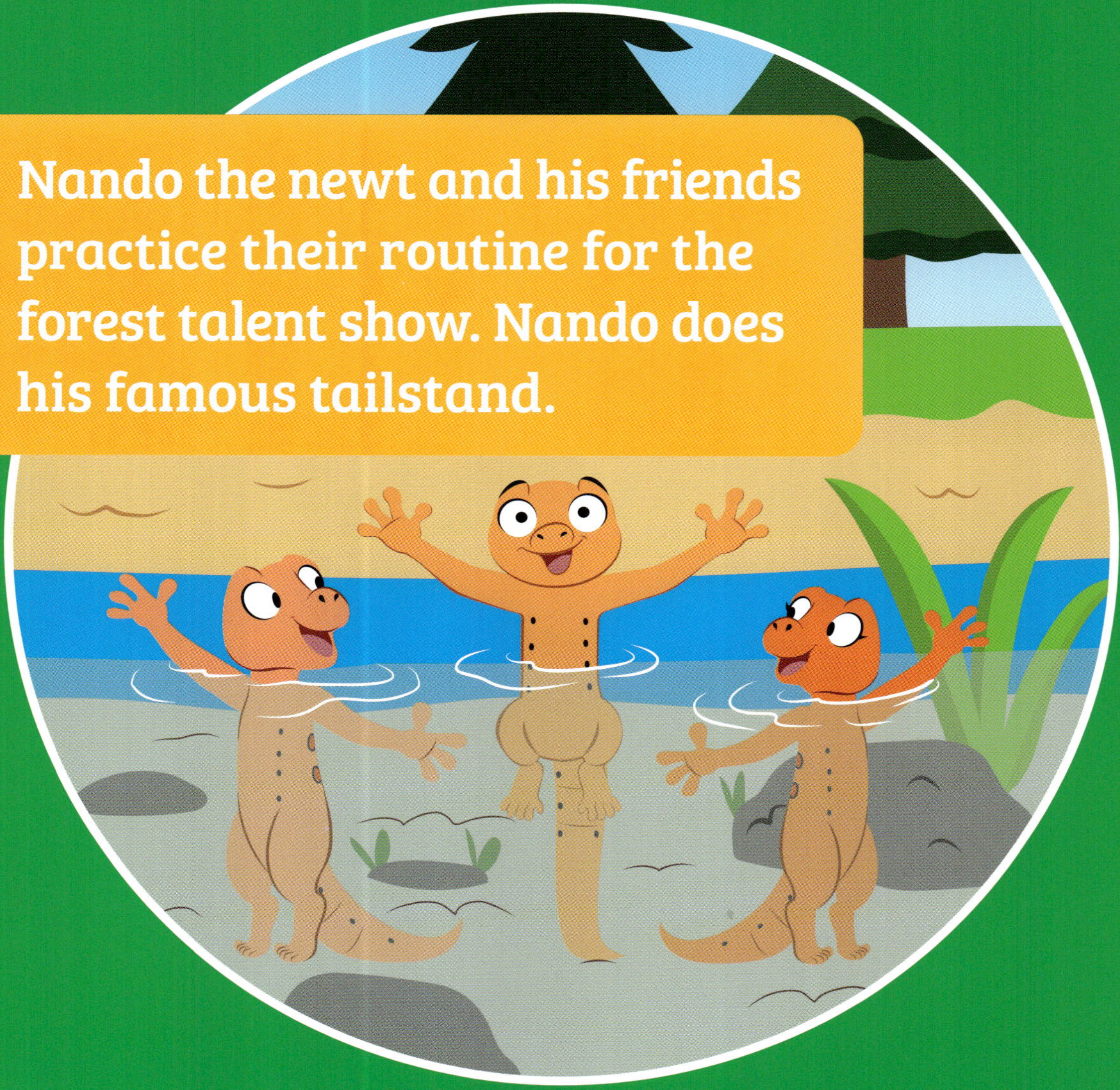

Nando the newt and his friends practice their routine for the forest talent show. Nando does his famous tailstand.

Nando, Natalie, and Nelly move their tails and arms together.

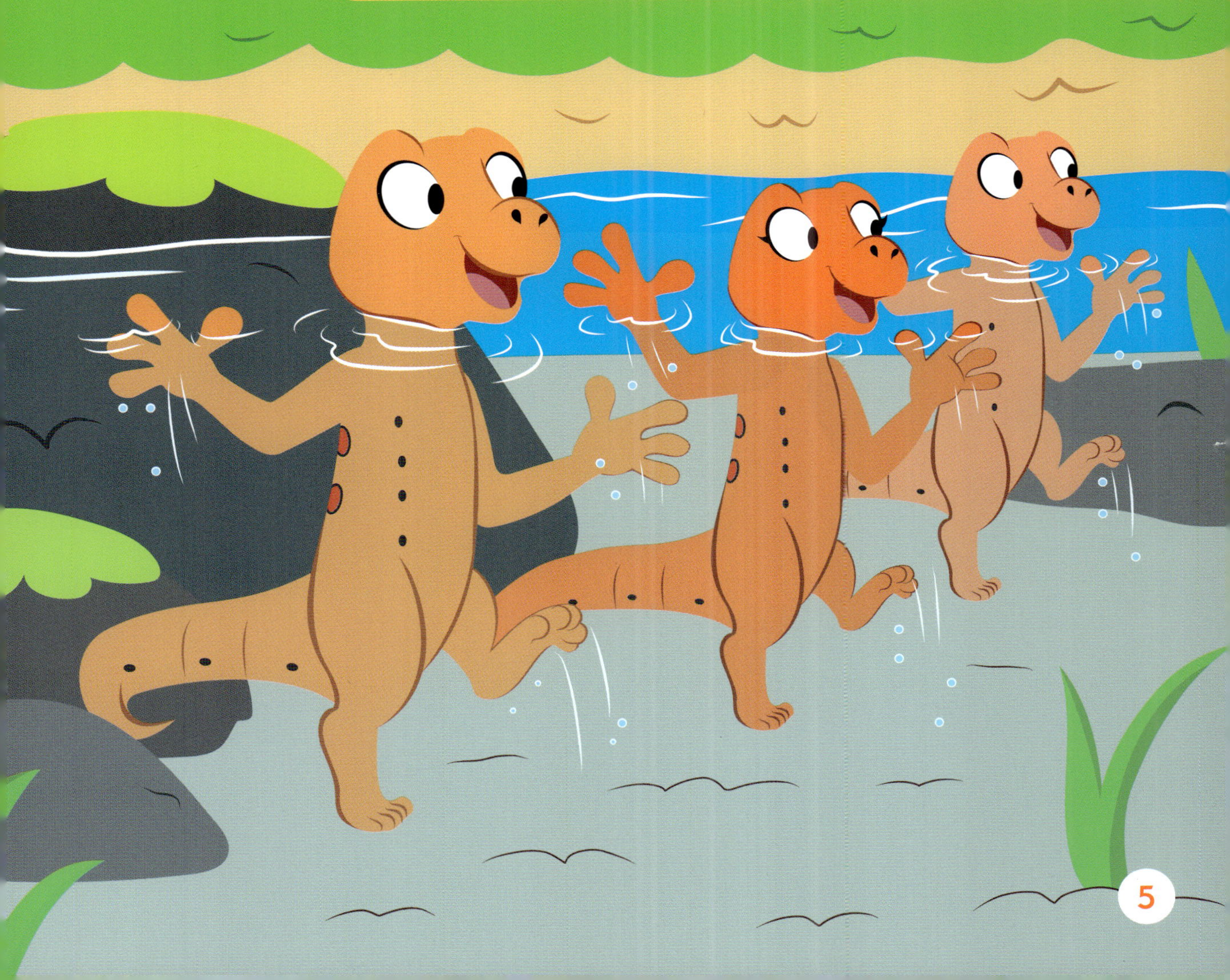

"And SPIN!" calls Natalie.

Natalie and Nelly finish their spins. But Nando's tail gets stuck between two rocks.

Nando pulls and pulls. He can't seem to break free!

POP! Nando's tail comes off!

"Help!" Nando screams as he scrambles onto a rock.

"What happened to your tail?!" Nelly yells.

Natalie is calm. She says, "You'll be OK, Nando. It will grow back. Remember when my brother lost his tail?"

Nando cries. The feeling inside him is shaky and hot. His heart beats fast. He breathes heavily.

"But what about our routine?" Nando worries. He wrings his hands. "What if my tail doesn't grow back in time? I won't be able to do my tailstand!"

“Take deep breaths like this,” Natalie says. She breathes in deeply and out slowly. Nando and Nelly do, too.

Nando’s breathing slows. His heart stops racing. But he still feels nervous.

"How will I do my tailstand for the talent show?" he asks.

"I have an idea!" Nelly says.
He whispers it to Nando.

The next day at the talent show, Nando feels a little nervous. His heart beats fast, but this time it's in a good way. He's excited to show off his new move.

Nando ends the routine in a handstand. His forest friends cheer. Nando forgets all about his nervous feelings.

Let's Review!

Look at the scenes below. Point to those that show Nando nervous. How do you know?

Picture Glossary

calm
Peaceful, soothing, and quiet.

routine
A performance that has been learned and practiced.

scrambles
Crawls or climbs very fast.

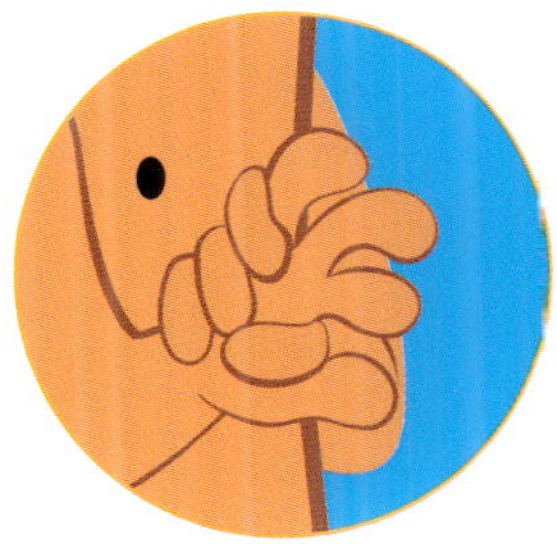

wrings
Rubs or twists one's hands together because they are nervous or upset.

Index

To Learn More

FACT SURFER

Finding more information is as easy as 1, 2, 3.

1. Go to www.factsurfer.com
2. Enter "**Nandothenewtfeelsnervous**" into the search box.
3. Choose your book to see a list of websites.